Red is a rainbow color.

Green sits next to blue.

Yellow, orange, violet, indigo,

they are rainbow colors, too, but

my color is *black* . . .

and there's

no BLACK

in rainbows.

Black is a **crayon**, tangled in a box.

Black is a **feather** on white winter snow.

Black is the **dirt** where sunflowers grow.

My color is black . . .

Black are the **braids** in my best friend's hair.

Black are the **bottoms of summertime feet.**

Black are **soft circles** that spin-nnn down the street.

My color is black.

Black is a rhythm.
Black is the blues.

Black is side-walking

in spit-shined shoes.

Celina
Wapakoneta
Kenton
Galion
Lexington
St. Marys
New Bremen
Russells Point
Marion
Mount Gilead
Centerburg
Fort Loramie
Anna
Jackson Center
Bellefontaine
Sidney
De Graff
West Liberty
Delaware
Marysville
Versailles
Ansonia
Covington
North Lewisburg
St. Paris
Urbana
Troy
Tipp City
New Carlisle
Arcanum
West Milton
Mechanicsburg
Northridge
Springfield
Columbus
West Jefferson
Grove City
London
Vandalia
Lewisburg
Utica
WASHINGTON
WAYNE
Athens
Leland
Indianola
Flora
Hattiesb
Petal
Brooklyn
Wiggins
DE SOTO NAT'L FOR.
Crosby

Black is the **robe** on Thurgood's back.

Black are the **trains** on railroad tracks.

Black are the **eyes** on salted peas.

Black are the **shadows** of ooo-old

magnolia trees.

Black is molasses from tall sugarcane.

Black is soft-singing,

"Hush now,

don't explain."

Black is the **skillet** for bread to fry.

Black are **dreams** and **raisins** . . .

left out

in the sun

to die.

ed and Talent
A Dream Deferr

Black is the color of ink staining page.
Black is the mask that shelters his rage.
Black are the birds in cages that sing—
Black is a color.
Black
is a culture.

Black is history. Black is family.

Black is memory. Black is community.

Black is the love that lives inside of me.

My color is Black.

Black are the stones bearing witness to prayer.

Black is the faith in a freedom not seen.

WE
DREAM.
HAVE
A

Black was the man

who gave the WORLD his dream.

Black is a color.

Black is a culture.

EQUAL
I AM
A MAN

Black is the heart of a candle and flame.

Black is the power of movement in pain.

Black are the branches that carry my name:

weaving, wrapping, lifting,

laughing, hoping, grasping, quiet,

strong.

Our color
is Black.

So you see,

there *is* no black in rainbows.

No black in green or blue.

But in my box of crayons,

Black is a rainbow, too.

Author's Note

On a chilly Tennessee evening, I gathered my children on the reading bench for what would be their first Black History Month lesson. The music I'd carefully selected was playing in the background. Age-appropriate picture books were on hand. Mental notes were sharp and inspired—I was ready. But before I could get a good start, my daughter looked at me with an air of preschool superiority and said, "But, Mama, we're not black, we're *brown*."

I was *not* prepared for that.

It was an innocent comment based on concrete observations. Indeed, our skin *is* brown. But her words revealed something that I had taken for granted: the understanding that Black is not just a color but a culture, too. I had work to do.

The word *black* can be dicey, though. Loaded with historical baggage, there are as many emotional responses to *black* as there are shades of tan, beige, and brown. Yet on these pages it has been my intent to present all that is beautiful, loving, and strong about *black* to make the word safe and palatable for children of all ethnicities. I hope that *Black Is a Rainbow Color* will serve as a point of departure for educators and parents alike, launching a greater exploration into this dynamic slice of American life and all of the complexities that go with it.

—Angela Joy

Black Is a Rainbow Color Playlist

"Homeless" - Ladysmith Black Mambazo with Paul Simon

"Lift Every Voice and Sing" - Committed

"Blowin' in the Wind" - Bob Dylan

"A Change Is Gonna Come" - Sam Cooke

"Say It Loud, I'm Black and I'm Proud" - James Brown

"To Be Young, Gifted and Black" - Nina Simone

"What's Going On" - Marvin Gaye

"Someday We'll All Be Free" - Donny Hathaway

"Shining Star" - Earth, Wind & Fire

"Blackbird" - Dionne Farris

"Glory" - John Legend and Common

More about *Black Is a Rainbow Color*

"SIDE-WALKING IN SPIT-SHINED SHOES": In 1955, following the arrest of Rosa Parks, the Black community of Montgomery, Alabama, collectively refused to ride in segregated buses. Instead, as a peaceful protest, they shined their most comfortable shoes and walked: to work, to school, to church. For 381 days they walked, until the local government, under legal and financial pressures, desegregated its buses allowing *all* passengers the freedom to sit in the seat of their choosing. As Dr. Martin Luther King Jr. later stated, "We came to see that, in the long run, it is more honorable to walk in dignity than ride in humiliation."

"ROBE ON THURGOOD'S BACK": Before becoming the first African American Supreme Court justice (1967–1991), Thurgood Marshall was a champion of the Civil Rights Movement. At times the *only* attorney for the NAACP, Marshall crisscrossed the nation serving Black clients who, without him, had little hope for adequate legal representation. One of his most influential cases, Brown v. Board of Education, asserted that racial segregation of children in public schools was a violation of the Fourteenth Amendment of the United States Constitution. The Supreme Court, in a unanimous decision, concluded that separate schools are "inherently unequal."

"TRAINS ON RAILROAD TRACKS": In Black art and literature, one will often encounter a train. The train may be literal: an homage, perhaps, to the six million Black Americans who boarded trains in order to flee southern poverty, violence, and oppression in what is called the Great Migration (1910–1970). Or, the train may be figurative: the "Heaven Bound Train" referred to in gospel songs and spirituals, or the Underground Railroad, led by "Conductor" Harriet Tubman—an escape route from enslavement that was neither underground nor a railroad. Trains in Black culture represent more than mere transportation. They symbolize the hopes and dreams of millions for an escape to freedom-land, found here on earth or on the other side.

"HUSH NOW, DON'T EXPLAIN": Among the many recordings of the melancholy melody "Don't Explain," there are two performances that stand out as the most requested. The first was released in 1946 by the composer herself, Billie Holiday (written with Arthur Herzog Jr.). The second is by activist and musician Nina Simone. It appears on her fifth album, *Let It All Out*. Both women achieve a level of raw vocal emotion that transcends race, language, and gender, making them ideal ambassadors of the Black experience worldwide.

"DREAMS AND RAISINS": In a poem titled "Harlem," (page 34) Langston Hughes compares unrealized dreams to raisins left out in the sun to shrivel and die—a metaphor so compelling, it inspired playwright Loraine Hansberry to use it as the title of her play, *A Raisin in the Sun*—the first African American play to be produced on Broadway (1959).

"BLACK IS THE COLOR OF INK STAINING PAGE": Despite being well-educated, African American author Paul Laurence Dunbar was not given access to employment that matched his intellect and skill. Racist hiring practices relegated him to work as an "elevator boy" at a Dayton, Ohio, bank in 1891. He wrote poetry while traffic was light. Two of his most famous poems are often quoted today: "We Wear the Mask" (page 34) and "Sympathy," (page 35) a work that inspired the title of Dr. Maya Angelou's first autobiography, *I Know Why the Caged Bird Sings.*

"STONES BEARING WITNESS TO PRAYER": In early masonry, cornerstones were the first stones set in construction. Upon these stones, all others were placed. Thus, cornerstones served as the foundation of the building. In the same way, the church has historically been the cornerstone—the foundation—of Black American life; a safe place for worshipers to pray, sing, socialize, and mourn. Seated at the unique intersection of spirituality and social activism, the Black church birthed the Civil Rights Movement. In its sanctuary, tens of thousands vowed to make change in honor of a boy named Emmett Till (Roberts Temple Church of God in Christ). In its basement, the Montgomery Bus Boycott was organized (Dexter Avenue Baptist Church). On its steps began three courageous marches toward the Edmund Pettus Bridge (Brown Chapel African Methodist Episcopal Church). These churches, and many like them, have served as the bedrock of the Black community, bearing witness to its hope, hurt, determination, and prayer.

Like cornerstones, Mamie Till-Mobley, Ella Baker, Marian Wright Edelman, and Fannie Lou Hamer set the foundation of the modern Civil Rights Movement: organizing coalitions, registering voters, riding for freedom, defending the poor. Under threat of physical and economic harm, these "Godmothers of the Movement" dared to sit in, stand up, and speak out, challenging the status quo and demanding equal rights on behalf of generations to come. While their names may not be well known, their contributions are woven deep within the tapestry of American history.

"THE MAN WHO GAVE THE WORLD HIS DREAM": Reverend Dr. Martin Luther King Jr. had a dream. A beautiful dream of hope, love, and equality for all. He spoke of his dream often, on platforms big and small. But when the time came for him to write the biggest speech of his life, he didn't include it. Perhaps he doubted the dream. Perhaps he was unsure of how a larger audience would receive it. Either way, Dr. King did not plan to talk about the dream that day. But as the March on Washington speech concluded (to what may be considered lukewarm applause), gospel singer Mahalia Jackson shouted from the crowd, "Tell them about the dream, Martin!" She knew the power of that dream. She knew what the hot and exhausted crowd needed: not just words, but inspiration. Trusting the instincts of Ms. Mahalia, Dr. King launched into what would become the most famous segment of his speech: "I have a dream . . ." Over time, Dr. King's dream became the dream of a nation; the hope of the world beyond.

Harlem (1951)

By Langston Hughes

What happens to a dream deferred?

Does it dry up
like a raisin in the sun?
Or fester like a sore—
And then run?
Does it stink like rotten meat?
Or crust and sugar over—
like a syrupy sweet?

Maybe it just sags
like a heavy load.

Or does it explode?

We Wear the Mask (1896)

By Paul Laurence Dunbar

We wear the mask that grins and lies,
It hides our cheeks and shades our eyes,—
This debt we pay to human guile;
With torn and bleeding hearts we smile,
And mouth with myriad subtleties.

Why should the world be overwise,
In counting all our tears and sighs?
Nay, let them only see us, while
We wear the mask.

We smile, but, O great Christ, our cries
To thee from tortured souls arise.
We sing, but oh the clay is vile
Beneath our feet, and long the mile;
But let the world dream otherwise,
We wear the mask!

Sympathy (1899)

By Paul Laurence Dunbar

I know what the caged bird feels, alas!
When the sun is bright on the upland slopes;
When the wind stirs soft through the springing grass,
And the river flows like a stream of glass;
When the first bird sings and the first bud opes,
And the faint perfume from its chalice steals—
I know what the caged bird feels!

I know why the caged bird beats his wing
Till its blood is red on the cruel bars;
For he must fly back to his perch and cling
When he fain would be on the bough a-swing;
And a pain still throbs in the old, old scars
And they pulse again with a keener sting—
I know why he beats his wing!

I know why the caged bird sings, ah me,
When his wing is bruised and his bosom sore,—
When he beats his bars and he would be free;
It is not a carol of joy or glee,
But a prayer that he sends from his heart's deep core,
But a plea, that upward to Heaven he flings—
I know why the caged bird sings!

Bound Together by Name

A Timeline of Black Ethnonyms in America

NEGRO—The first enslaved people from Africa arrived in the United States in 1619. They were called negro by their captors, a derogatory classification that stripped them of name, tribe, and nationality, reducing them to merely a color—the Spanish word for "black."

HYPODESCENDANT—Also known as the "one-drop rule." In 1705, presumably in response to the birth of Afro-European children, Virginia passed legislation defining a "negro" not by appearance but by ancestry. Regardless of hue, any person who was the child, grandchild, or great-grandchild of a negro was considered negro. In South Carolina, the classification extended even further to include great-great-grandchildren. These laws actively prohibited individuals with mixed heritage from claiming the rights and freedoms of their white foreparents.

AFRICAN—In 1787, the Free African Society was formed in the United States. The organization later birthed the African Methodist Episcopal (AME) church—the largest Protestant denomination founded by Black people in the world. Pride of heritage led them to their chosen designation, *African*.

AFRO-AMERICAN—The year 1887 brought the founding of the National Afro-American League. This term, claiming both African and American nationhood, has come in and out of fashion over time, yet has failed to become a cultural staple.

NEGRO—In a footnote of his 1899 publication, *The Philadelphia Negro: A Social Study*, activist, educator, and author W. E. B. Du Bois quietly began a decades-long campaign to capitalize the *N* in "negro." He wrote, in part, "I believe that eight million Americans are entitled to a capital letter." In an editorial appearing on March 7, 1930, the *New York Times* agreed, changing its "style book" accordingly.

COLORED—In 1909, the National Association for the Advancement of Colored People (NAACP) was founded. By this time, the term *colored* was widespread. Used to include those of mixed heritage, the designation distanced Black people from the negative stereotypes then being associated with the term *African*.

THE "SO-CALLED" NEGRO—Mid-1950s. This phrase was used by religious leaders and activists such as Adam Clayton Powell Jr. and Elijah Muhammad to summarily reject the term *Negro*, associating it with Black subservience or passivity.

BLACK —By the early 1960s, the ethnonym *Black* was being used boldly to embrace a distinct heritage and identity. Adopted by high-profile figures such as Malcolm X, Stokely Carmichael, and James Brown, phrases such as "Black Power," "Black History," and "Black Pride" were popularized and integrated into the cultural norm. In 1966, the Black Panther Party for Self-Defense was established: a political party dedicated to the protection and empowerment of the Black community.

AFRICAN-AMERICAN—In December 1988, Reverend Jesse Jackson called a press conference to announce an alternate designation for Americans of African descent: *African-American*. He asserted that being called African-American "puts us in our proper historical context." The U.S. Census Bureau added the option next to "black" in the year 2000.

BLACK IS BACK—Despite the popularity of *African-American*, *Black* is still used to self-describe people of African descent, as evidenced by organizations such as Black Girls Rock! (2006) and Black Lives Matter (2013).

2020—Common standards of writing practice call for the use of a lowercase *b* when referring to Black people and their interests. In the spirit of the W. E. B. Du Bois campaign, the *B* in "Black" has been capitalized herein.

For children who ask difficult questions,
and adults who brave the unknown
for answers —A.J.

To all of my family, the most beautiful
rainbow I know —E.H.

Bibliography

Amira, Dan. "15 Things You Might Not Know About the 'I Have a Dream' Speech." Daily Intelligencer, August 28, 2013, nymag.com/intelligencer/2013/08/i-have-a-dream-speech-facts-trivia.html.

Bennett, Jr., Lerone. "What's In a Name? Negro vs. Afro-American vs. Black." *Ebony Magazine*, November 1967, virginia.edu/woodson/courses/aas102%20(spring%2001)/articlesnames bennett.html.

Du Bois, W. E. Burghardt. *The Philadelphia Negro: A Social Study*. Ginn & Co., 1899. Page 1.

Dunbar, Paul Laurence. "Sympathy." In *Selected Poems: Paul Laurence Dunbar*, edited by Glenn Mott, 28. Mineola: Dover Publications, Inc., 1997.

Dunbar, Paul Laurence. "We Wear the Mask." In *Selected Poems: Paul Laurence Dunbar*, edited by Glenn Mott, 17–18. Mineola: Dover Publications, Inc., 1997.

Editorial. "'Negro' With a Capital 'N.'" *The New York Times*, March 7, 1930.

Gentry, Tony. *Paul Laurence Dunbar, Poet*. New York: Chelsea House Publishers, 1989.

Hughes, Langston. "Harlem [2]." In *The Collected Poems of Langston Hughes*, edited by Arnold Rampersad, 426. New York: Alfred A. Knopf, Inc., 1994.

King Jr., Martin Luther. *The Papers of Martin Luther King, Jr., Volume III: Birth of a New Age*, December 1955–December 1956. First ed. Berkeley: University of California Press, 1997. Page 486.

Tharps, Lori L. "The Case for Black With a Capital B." *The New York Times*, November 18, 2014, nytimes.com/2014/11/19/opinion/the-case-for-black-with-a-capital-b.html.